Fantasy Quest

The Catacombs of Chaos

About the author

David J H Smith was originally from Slough, Berkshire but is now living in Somerset.

He graduated from Thames Valley University with an Honours Degree in History & Geography before going on to study History at Post Graduate level at Westminster University.

David has worked in various jobs such as Immigration, Retail Manager, Facilities Officer and IT before becoming a writer and setting up 'Things From Dimension - X' which specialises in the sale of rare and collectable comic books.

Other Works:

The Titanic's Mummy

Sensational Tales

Fantasy Quests

The Catacombs of Chaos

By

David J H Smith

Paige Croft Publishing

Paige Croft Publishing, Yeovil, Somerset

David J H Smith asserts the moral right to be identified as the author of this work

Cover Template by Jo Stroud
Main Cover Image - The Catacombs of Chaos

Incidental Art - Public Domain Clipart

Nov 2020

Published by Paige Croft Publishing

All rights reserved. No part of this publication may be reproduced, stored in a retrieval system, or transmitted, in any form or by any means: electronic, mechanical, photocopying, recording or otherwise, without the prior permission of the publisher.

This book is sold subject to the condition that it shall not, by way of trade or otherwise, be lent, re-sold, hired out or otherwise circulated without the authors prior consent in any form or binding other than that in which it is published and without a similar condition including this condition being imposed on the subsequent purchaser

Introduction

'Fantasy Quests' are Solo Roleplay Gamebooks, where you take on the role of the hero.

After creating your character you will navigate your way through the adventure until either you complete the quest, or you perish in the attempt.

Game Equipment Required

To play the game, apart from this book, you will need a pencil, eraser and a traditional six sided die.

Adventure Chart Instructions

Details of your character and items carried are written down on the Adventure Chart section of this book. You can of course make copies of this chart for later use but if you decide to write within the book itself, please ensure that you write on it lightly in pencil so you can erase the details later.

Character Setup

Before you start your adventure you must setup and equip your character and enter these details on the Adventure Chart Section of the book.

Health:

Roll the die and add 20 to this number then record this in the Health section on your Adventure Chart. During your adventure your health will constantly change. If at any time your health score reaches 0 or less, you have been killed and your adventure is over. You will be given the chance to regain lost points, but your Health may never exceed your initial total.

Combat Skill:

Roll the die and add 6 to it. Enter this number in the Combat Skill section of your Adventure Chart. This is your basic Combat Skill which determines your fighting ability. During your adventure you will have the chance to add to this number by picking up weapons and specialized equipment.

Clothes and Equipment

Clothes:

You are dressed in leather armour, breeches and knee high leather boots.

Equipment:

You start your adventure with the following equipment:

Rucksack:

It is slung over your shoulder. This canvas rucksack is where you will store your food, potions and magical items.

Weapons:

Initially you are armed with a sword (add this to your Adventure Chart and 1 point to your Combat Skill).

During your quest you will be given the opportunity to acquire other weapons, some with magical properties, which will add to your initial Combat Skill. You will be given instructions on how to use them in the numbered sections.

You can carry a maximum of two weapons at a time, but can only use one in combat. Before combat choose the most appropriate weapon for the encounter and make any alterations to your Combat Skill. (E.G. A fire sword would be useless against a Fire Sprite, but would be the perfect weapon against a Snow Demon).

Meals:

You start with 3 meals (Add this to your Adventure Chart in the section marked Meals) but it may be possible for you to pick up other meals and foodstuffs during your adventure to either eat straight away or keep for later. You may eat a meal at the end of the action on the numbered sections, before you go onto the next - unless of course it is clear that the action is ongoing into the next section.

When you eat a meal you can add 2 to your Health but can only eat one meal per numbered section, and when you do so you must cross it off your Adventure Chart.

Potions:

It is possible you may come across various potions. You will be instructed on what they do when you find them. You can either take a potion straight away or keep it for later. If you are keeping it for later, remember to mark it on your Adventure Chart and then cross it off once used. Again, like meals and water, you can only take a potion at the end of a numbered section unless of course it is clear that the action is ongoing into the next section.

Magical Items:

Although you are not trained in magic you may have the opportunity to pick up magical items or spells. Record the items and how to use them in the Magic section of your Adventure Chart.

Gameplay

Navigation:

You navigate your way through this adventure by using the die and the Navigation Grid.

Roll the die once and this number will relate to the 1 - 6 at the top of the chart.

Roll the die again and this will relate to the 1 - 6 on the side of the chart.

Use these numbers as co-ordinates to see which numbered section of the book you must turn to.

Combat:

During the adventure you are very likely to come across an enemy who you will have to fight.

Details of the encounter are filled in on the Combat Table within the text, which will already give you your enemy's Combat Skill. Again, like the Adventure Chart, make sure this is filled in lightly in pencil so it can be erased.

The steps for Combat are as follows:

1 - Roll the die and add this to your Enemy's Combat Skill

2 - This number is their Combat Total - record this down on the Table

3 - On the Table record your Combat Skill (including any bonuses).

4 - Roll the die and add this to your Combat Skill to give you your Combat Total and record this down.

5 - Compare the two Combat Totals.

6 - If your Combat Total is equal or higher than your enemy you have won the combat and your enemy is dead and you must now see what damage they have managed to inflict on you during the fight. To do this roll the die and take this number away from your Health.

If you are still alive, erase the details of this encounter on the Combat Table, and continue the adventure as directed by the text.

7 - If, however, your enemy's Combat Total was higher, they have beaten you and your life and adventure ends here.

Hazards:

During the adventure you will come across various traps and hazards that you will have to negotiate. To get passed them you will be required to roll the die and check the outcome on the Hazard Results Table within the section. Sometimes you will be able to add bonuses to the die roll through weapons or other items carried.

BACKGROUND STORY

You stare down at the bowl of 'Boar Meat Stew' that the tavern's serving girl placed before you a few moments earlier. It doesn't look or taste right. Sadly, you are familiar with the taste of cooked rat and have a sneaking suspicion that that is what you have just eaten.

You are about to get up and complain, when a large tankard of honeyed milk is placed directly in front of you. On looking up, you see your benefactor is an old man with a long white beard wearing a hooded cloak and holding a wooden staff. You nod your thanks and he takes the empty seat directly in front of you. "I have eaten here before," he explains. "You will need that to line your stomach so you don't throw up as well as taking away the taste of the food."

"Thank you," you reply gratefully, "rat leaves a terrible aftertaste, no matter how well it's cooked."

"Rat?" queries the old man, with a smile. "Rat? You think that's rat you're eating? Oh my dear boy, you are optimistic!"

You hurriedly push the bowl away and take a large swig from the tankard before placing it back down again. "Forgive my suspicion old man," you say, trying not to think about what meat you have just eaten, "but normally when a stranger gives you a drink in a tavern it's because they are after something."

"And this is no exception," replies the old man honestly. "I understand that you are a sword for hire."

"One of the best in the land," you say proudly. "Three years in the King's Guard and another two freelance."

"Good," said the old man, "because I am in need of your skills urgently. Oh, by the way, let me introduce myself, I am Magnus."

"Magnus? Not *the* Magnus?" you reply in surprise: "Wizard to the Kings and one of the most powerful mages in the Kingdom? The eternal man who has walked the earth for a thousand years? Slayer of the black Dragon? Guardian of the Portal of Mayers?"

"I'm afraid the bards have been over generous in their description," he says, almost uncomfortably. "But, yes, I am he."

"What on earth could you want with me?" you ask in surprise.

"I have a specific issue that needs addressing and I cannot do it on my own," replies Magnus. "You are of course familiar with the story of Baron Braxe?"

You nod. The story of the Baron and his demise was a well-known tale. Braxe was known for his cruelty and greed but then, in his quest for power, he turned to the use of the forbidden dark magic. Quickly, rumours began to spread about strange sightings of undead creatures and macabre practices being carried out at the Baron's ancestral mansion. Then girls from the nearby village began to disappear. It was at that point it was decided that something had to be done and a heroic band of heroes, led by Magnus, launched a successful assault where the Baron was killed and the mansion was razed to the ground.

"Well it seems that The Baron is not as dead as I had hoped," explained Magnus. "It appears he has managed to rise up from his grave and is planning to renew his activities. He needs to be stopped and the only way to do that is to venture down into the catacombs under what is left of the mansion."

"Which is where I come in I assume?" you ask.

Magnus nods. "I'm prevented from going in there due to various binding spells so I need help: someone to go in and finish the job once and for all."

As a seasoned adventurer you have taken on 'Dungeon Crawls' before; going into dungeons, tombs and catacombs, negotiating booby traps and of course fighting whatever creatures are lurking there. It's dangerous and unforgiving work. The last one you undertook nearly cost you your life and your sanity, so embarking on another is not that appealing to you. "I seem to recall the Baron was killed by an enchanted sword and the story goes it was snapped into two pieces?"

"Yes, that's right," confirms Magnus. "It was charmed with specific spells to counteract the magic he was using and is the only weapon that can be used to defeat him. Both pieces are somewhere in the catacombs. You will have to find them before you take on the Baron. The magic the sword bears means it will automatically fix itself when the two pieces are placed together."

You pause, taking in the enormity of the task presented to you. Then something occurs to you. "Am I the first adventurer you have approached for this?"

"No," replies Magnus bluntly. "You are the fourth. All the others refused."

You are about to shake your head and decline when Magnus reaches into his cloak, pulls out a small leather pouch and drops it on the table in front of you. "If you agree to help, and survive, this will be your reward."

You reach for the small bag and open it to see that it is filled with gold and silver nuggets as well as various gems. It is a fortune that could easily last you for the rest of your life - or a very enjoyable six months. You close the bag and then, against your better judgment, find yourself nodding your head: agreeing to take on the quest.

The next morning you meet Magnus outside the Tavern and the two of you head off to what is left of the Baron's Mansion. After half a day's ride you come to a gatehouse, where you abandon your mounts and head up the narrowing path on foot. With every step you take, you feel the air get heavier and the atmosphere darken with a terrible foreboding. Eventually, you come to a large clearing and the sight that greets you fills you with horror and morbid fascination. Despite the fact that the Baron's mansion was destroyed a year ago, the ruin that you expected to see is not there. Instead, you are confronted with a building site, and the workers involved are living skeletons.

"This is as I feared," said Magnus. "The Baron is rebuilding and, by the looks of things, it won't be a mere house but a fortified stronghold."

One of the skeletons looks up and notices you. Your hand moves to your sword but Magnus stops you, explaining that they will not harm you unless you try to harm them. He hurries you on past the building work before suddenly stopping. "This is the entrance to the catacombs," he explains, as he waves his hand and the flagstone lifts to reveal a shallow slope leading down into a dimly lit tunnel. "I can't go down there due to the binding spells. From now on you will be on your own."

"Understood," you reply apprehensively.

"There is some help I can give you though," he continues, reaching into his robe. First he hands you a red stone the size of a large die. He explains that it is a Translocation Stone. Should you encounter Baron Braxe before you have found both pieces of the sword you can use it to teleport yourself away (you will be given this option in the text.) Magnus then warns you that it will only be able to be used ONCE. You take the small stone and place it in your pocket (Add this to your Adventure Chart in the Magic section). Magnus then takes your sword and passes his hand over it, enchanting it. When used in combat it now adds 1 point to your Combat Skill (mark this on your Adventure Chart). You take the weapon back and replace it into its scabbard. Finally he hands you a small vial containing a blue liquid, explaining that it is a Health potion. When you choose to drink it, it will restore 8 Health Points (mark this on your Adventure Chart).

"Now remember," warns Magnus, "the Baron must be destroyed at all costs or I have no idea what havoc he could cause."

And with that you cautiously head down the slope into the catacombs until you find yourself in a long passageway; the floor is lined with flagstones and, at regular intervals, set into the roughly cut stone walls, are blazing torches lighting your way. There is a smell of death and decay hanging in the air along with a feeling of something more sinister awaiting you.

You grip your sword tightly as you move forward, wondering if you will ever make it out alive.

Now turn to the Navigation Grid to begin your adventure ......

Adventure Chart

Health:

Combat Skill:

Weapons (With Bonuses):

Magnus's Sword:

    Hilt & Guard: Main Blade:

Meals (+2 HEALTH POINTS PER MEAL - ONE MEAL PER NUMBERED SECTION):

Equipment:

Magic Items & Potions:

Navigation Grid

	1	2	3	4	5	6
1	12	28	9	23	15	36
2	35	6	26	2	31	19
3	17	1	14	37	11	25
4	32	13	8	21	29	5
5	7	22	38	18	3	24
6	39	4	27	33	16	34

Numbered Sections

~ 1 ~

You enter a section of the catacombs where, set into the walls, there are a series of horizontal alcoves containing skeletons.

A particular one catches your eye, for it is holding a small scroll which, on investigation, you discover is a healing spell.

Roll the die to see how many Health Points it will restore when you choose to take it.

Alter your Adventure Chart accordingly and then return to the Navigation Grid to continue your adventure.

~ 2 ~

Swinging back and forth across this section of the catacomb are three large bladed pendulums which you will have to run past.

Roll the die to see if you make it past the blades.

Number Rolled	Outcome
1	- 2 Health Points
2 or 3	- 4 Health Points
4 or 5	- 6 Health Points
6	No Damage Taken

If you survive, return to the Navigation Grid to continue your adventure.

~ 3 ~

You enter into a section of the catacombs lined with horizontal alcoves, each containing bodies in various states of decomposition. The smell of death is almost overwhelming (Lose 1 Health Point). Then, to your horror and surprise, one of the corpses rolls out of its alcove onto the floor in front of you before getting up and stumbling towards you, its arms outstretched.

You must fight this undead creature.

Corpse's Combat Skill	8
Corpse's Combat Total	
My Combat Skill	
My Combat Total	

If you survive the combat, return to the Navigation Grid to continue your adventure.

~ 4 ~

Bubbling up from the floor you find a fresh water spring and take a drink. Restore 2 Health Points and then continue your adventure by returning to the Navigation Grid.

~ 5 ~

You suddenly feel a light breeze which, within moments, becomes a strong, sustained gust, which passes through the section of the catacombs over you. As you struggle to stay upright debris flies at you and hits you.

Roll the die to see how much damage you take.

Number Rolled	Outcome
1 or 2	- 4 Health Points
3	- 2 Health Points
4	No Damage Taken
5 or 6	- 6 Health Points

If you are still alive the wind dies down and you are able to continue onwards

Return to the Navigation Grid to continue your adventure.

~ 6 ~

Rounding the tunnel's corner you find a hooded figure with red glowing eyes, dressed in brown robes, armed with a scythe. You recognise it as the Crypt Guardian, a creature used to protect tombs and vaults from intruders. As it moves into attack, you ready yourself for combat.

Crypt Guardian's Combat Skill	10
Crypt Guardian's Combat Total	
My Combat Skill	
My Combat Total	

If you win against the Crypt Guardian its scythe disappears into a pile of ash. Return to the Navigation Grid to continue your adventure.

~ 7 ~

Feeling tired from your efforts so far you decide to sit down and rest for a few minutes.

Add 3 to your Health Points.

Return to the Navigation Grid to continue your adventure.

~ 8 ~

From above, you hear an ominous cracking sound and, looking up, you see a large section of the cavern roof starting to crack and fracture and you find yourself showered with debris.

Roll the die to see how badly you are injured, if at all.

Number Rolled	Outcome
1 or 2	- 3 Health Points
3	No Damage Taken
4 or 5	- 6 Health Points
6	- 2 Health Point

If you are still alive, return to the Navigation Grid to continue your adventure.

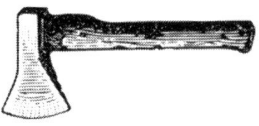

~ 9 ~

As you continue, you notice a small bunch of pink mushrooms growing against the side of the passageway wall. You recognise them as safe to eat and pick them immediately.

The mushrooms will restore 4 Health Points. If you decide not to eat them straight away, you place them in your rucksack to have later.

Alter your Adventure Chart accordingly and then continue your adventure by returning to the Navigation Grid.

~ 10 ~

Your hand reaches for the Translocation Stone that Magnus gave you at the start of this adventure: for now is not the time for you to face down the Baron, to do so would mean certain death.

As if understanding what is required of it, the stone begins to glow and you find yourself enveloped in a strange light. When it subsides you find yourself no longer in the Baron's chamber of the dead, but standing in a passage somewhere in the catacombs. You breathe a sigh of relief, place the magical stone back in your pocket, making a mental note that if you get out of this alive you will thank Magnus for his foresight.

Turn to Numbered Section 27 and continue your adventure.

~ 11 ~

Etched onto the stone wall you notice a strange inscription, which you translate as the word 'renewal'. You place your hand on this mark and feel a warm surge run through your entire body. When you remove your hand the mark is gone.

Roll the die to see how many Health Points you recover and then continue your adventure by returning to the Navigation Grid.

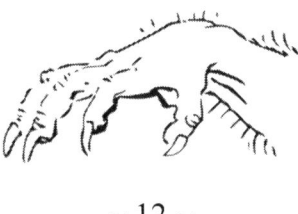

~ 12 ~

Running along the tunnel ceiling and walls are a mass of tangled tree roots. As you get closer they come to life and lunge out at you. You must fight your way past them.

Tree Roots Combat Skill	6
Tree Roots Combat Total	
My Combat Skill	
My Combat Total	

If you survive the combat, return to the Navigation Grid to continue your adventure.

~ 13 ~

The passageway splits into two. With no clear indication as to which path you should take, you decide to take the right fork.

Return to the Navigation Grid to continue your adventure.

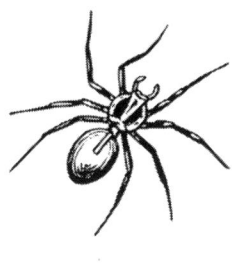

~ 14 ~

Across this section of the tunnel is a strange shimmering portal which you must walk through. As you do so you feel your body being engulfed by pain.

Roll the die to see how badly you are injured, if at all.

Number Rolled	Outcome
1	No Damage Taken
2 or 3	- 2 Health Points
4	- 8 Health Points
5 or 6	- 4 Health Points

If you survive, return to the Navigation Grid to continue your adventure.

~ 15 ~

If this is the first time that you have come to this section continue reading. If you have come to this section before, return to the Navigation Grid to continue your adventure.

Stumbling towards you is a headless man dressed in leather armour similar to that of your own. Clutched in his right hand is the handle and guard of a broken sword. You realise at once that this must be one of the heroes who, led by Magnus, originally tried to stop the Baron. The sword he is holding is part of the one you have been searching for.

As he gets closer he lashes out at you and you dodge out of the way, the remains of the weapon barely missing you. With no alternative you ready yourself for battle.

Adventurer's Combat Skill	9
Adventurer's Combat Total	
My Combat Skill	
My Combat Total	

If you survive the combat, take the remains of Magnus's sword from the hand of the fallen adventurer. If you now have both pieces of the weapon turn straight to Section 20. If not, place the handle & guard onto your rucksack (mark this down in the Adventure Chart) and then return to the Navigation Grid to continue on your adventure.

~ 16 ~

Without any warning, a hand grabs you, from behind, on the shoulder and you feel a sudden pain in the centre of your back. You gasp and look down to see the point of a sword sticking out of your chest and then become aware of a face close to yours. "Sent by Magnus, I presume, to stop me?" hisses Baron Braxe into your ear. "Well you failed on that score didn't you?" In one fluid move he then twists the sword, pulls it free and steps back.

You collapse into a heap on the floor and, as everything begins to go dark, the tunnel is filled by the triumphant laughter of the Baron.

Your adventure ends here.

~ 17 ~

You come across a shallow pool of ankle deep bubbling water that stretches out in front of you for twenty feet. To reach the other side you will have no option but to run through it and will no doubt be scolded in the process.

Roll the die to see how badly you are injured, if at all.

Number Rolled	Outcome
1	- 2 Health Points
2 or 3	- 4 Health Points
4 or 5	- 6 Health Points
6	No Damage Taken

If you are still alive, return to the Navigation Grid to continue your adventure.

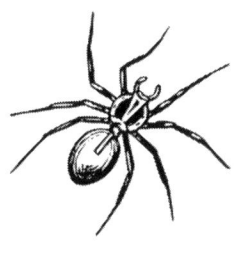

~ 18 ~

You enter a section of the catacombs where, set into the walls, there are a series of horizontal alcoves containing skeletons: one of which is holding a golden mace. On closer inspection you realise the weapon has magical properties.

Roll the die once - this is the amount the weapon will add to your Combat Skill. In addition it will reduce any damage you take in battle by 3 when used in battle.

If you take the mace, note these properties down on your Adventure Chart before continuing your adventure by returning to the Navigation Grid.

~ 19 ~

You find yourself being approached by a young man brandishing a sword. On seeing his ordinary looking clothes and the strange distant look in his eyes you realise that this must be one of the villagers that have been taken and enslaved by the Baron.

As he moves into attack, you reluctantly ready yourself for battle.

Villager's Combat Skill	8
Villager's Combat Total	
My Combat Skill	
My Combat Total	

If you survive the combat, return to the Navigation Grid to continue your adventure.

~ 20 ~

From your rucksack you take the other piece of the broken sword and place it, along with the piece you have just found, on the floor close together. Immediately both pieces of the weapon start to glow brightly, forcing you to shield your eyes. After a few moments the light subsides and you see that the sword has now magically fused itself together just as Magnus promised. Instinctively you reach out and pick up the weapon. It is like no sword you have ever held before: light, perfectly balanced with a blade that is beyond razor sharp.

Then the residual magic that mended the sword passes over you and your whole body is enveloped in a warm glow.

Restore your Heath Points to their original total. Smiling, you place Magnus's sword in your belt, relieved that you have managed to find it.

The Sword adds 8 points to your original Combat Skill and will also reduce any damage you receive in battle by 3 points.

As the power of Magnus's sword is so strong and that this is the weapon that you will ultimately use against the Baron, you decide to leave all other weapons behind and will not pick any more up on the remainder of your time in the catacombs. (Cross any existing weapons off your Adventure Chart.)

Turn to Numbered Section 27 to continue your adventure.

~ 21 ~

From above, you hear a flapping sound; you look up to see a small swarm of bats flying straight towards you. As they pass over they attack you. You must try to fend them off as one enemy.

Bats Combat Skill	7
Bats Combat Total	
My Combat Skill	
My Combat Total	

If you survive the combat, return to the Navigation Grid to continue your adventure.

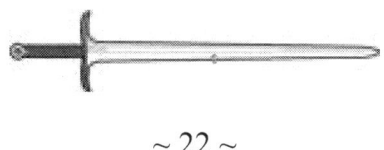

~ 22 ~

You stand on a hidden pressure pad and, from a hole in the wall a crossbow bolt is shot out. With no time to react the bolt hits you.

Roll the die to see how badly you are injured and deduct this from your health.

Number Rolled	Outcome
1 or 2	- 4 Health Points
3	- 2 Health Points
4	No Damage Taken
5 or 6	- 6 Health Points

If you survive, you pull out the bolt from your body and throw it to one side and then return to the Navigation Grid to continue your adventure.

~ 23 ~

The passageway splits into two. With no clear indication as to which path you should take, you decide to take the left fork.

Return to the Navigation Grid to continue your adventure.

~ 24 ~

Lying on the floor you find an abandoned rucksack. On opening it you find the following: Two meals, and a small vial of healing potion that will restore 3 health points when you choose to take it.

Alter your Adventure Chart accordingly before continuing on your way by returning to the Navigation Grid.

~ 25 ~

The passageway opens up into a large rounded chamber, the walls of which are lined by bodies in varying states of decay set into roughly carved alcoves. At the centre of the room are steps leading up to a large throne which appears to be made entirely out of skulls. On this sits a man dressed in black metal armour, Baron Braxe. Beside him there is a large black dog with one eye in the middle of its head who is growling expectantly.

If this is the first time you have encountered Baron Braxe and wish to avoid the impending combat (as you have not yet recovered Magnus's Sword) you can make use of the Translocation Stone by turning immediately to Numbered Section 10. Otherwise read on)

The Baron looks you up and down with contempt and, in a raspy voice, utters the word, "Attack!" In response, the one eyed dog advances towards you.

You must fight this creature.

Attack Dog's Combat Skill	14
Attack Dog's Combat Total	
My Combat Skill	
My Combat Total	

If you survive the combat, turn to Section 30.

~ 26 ~

From the ceiling a giant spider, the size of a goat, drops down and lands on the floor in front of you. It rears up and then launches itself at you.

Giant Spider's Combat Skill	7
Giant Spider's Combat Total	
My Combat Skill	
My Combat Total	

If you survive the combat, return to the Navigation Grid to continue your adventure.

~ 27 ~

Adjusting your rucksack, you continue onwards, working your way through the catacombs without incident.

Return to the Navigation Grid to continue your adventure.

~ 28 ~

In this section of corridor you see spears randomly shooting out from the walls at various heights before retracting back in again.

You run through the spears dodging and weaving as you go. Roll the die to see if you are injured or not.

Number Rolled	Outcome
1 or 2	- 3 Health Points
3	No Damage Taken
4 or 5	- 6 Health Points
6	- 2 Health Point

If you are still alive, return to the Navigation Grid to continue your adventure.

~ 29 ~

The tunnel abruptly splits into two. You opt to take the left fork.

Return to the Navigation Grid to continue your adventure.

~ 30 ~

You stare down at the dead attack dog on the floor before turning your attention to the Baron himself, who nods to you in respect. He stands and pulls out, from the scabbard on his belt, a large sword which immediately catches fire. He then slowly, almost casually, descends the steps of his throne and advances towards you.

This is the moment you have been waiting for: the final encounter with Baron Braxe. Taking a deep breath to steady yourself you brace yourself for combat.

Baron Braxe's Combat Skill	16
Baron Braxe's Combat Total	
My Combat Skill	
My Combat Total	

If you defeat the Baron and survive the combat, turn to Numbered Section 40.

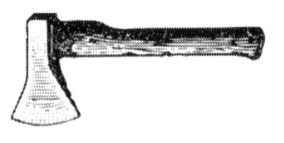

~ 31 ~

Feeling fatigued, you decide to stop and rest for a moment.

Add 3 to your Health then return to the Navigation Grid to continue your adventure.

~ 32 ~

Out of the shadows steps a Dark Elf who moves in to attack you. With no option you ready yourself for battle.

Dark Elf's Combat Skill	11
Dark Elf's Combat Total	
My Combat Skill	
My Combat Total	

If you survive, you search the body and discover two potions of healing which will restore 3 Health Points when you drink them. Mark these down on your Adventure Chart. You may also take his silver sword. Roll the die once - this is the amount the weapon will add to your Combat Skill. In addition it will also reduce any damage you take in combat by 2 points.

Alter your Adventure Chart accordingly and then return to the Navigation Grid to continue your adventure.

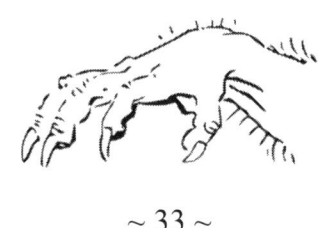

~ 33 ~

As you are walking along, from the wall of the catacomb, two mummified hands reach out and grab you around the throat and start to strangle you. Using all your strength you pull yourself free.

Roll the die to see how badly you are injured, if at all.

Number Rolled	Outcome
1	No Damage Taken
2 or 3	- 2 Health Points
4	- 8 Health Points
5 or 6	- 4 Health Points

If you are still alive, return to the Navigation Grid to continue your adventure.

~ 34 ~

Turning the corner you suddenly find yourself confronted with a skeleton armed with a rusty sword. On seeing you the undead creature slowly advances towards you. You ready yourself for combat.

Skeleton's Combat Skill	8
Skeleton's Combat Total	
My Combat Skill	
My Combat Total	

42

If you survive the combat, return to the Navigation Grid to continue your adventure.

~ 35 ~

If this is the first time that you have come to this section continue reading. If you have come to this section before, return to the Navigation Grid to continue your adventure.

In the middle of the corridor you see a block of stone from which is protruding the remains of a blade which you instantly realise must be part of Magnus's sword. You grab it and pull it free, but as you do so it cuts into your hand. (Roll 1 die and deduct this number from your Health).

If you now have both pieces of Magnus's sword turn straight to Section 20. If not, you place the blade into your rucksack (mark this down in the Adventure Chart) and then return to the Navigation Grid to continue on your adventure.

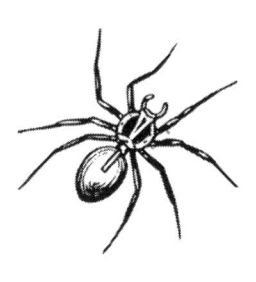

~ 36 ~

From above, you hear a strange hissing sound and then find yourself momentarily engulfed in a steam jet.

Roll the die to see how many Health Points you must deduct from your total.

Number Rolled	Outcome
1	- 2 Health Points
2 or 3	- 4 Health Points
4 or 5	- 6 Health Points
6	No Damage Taken

If you are still alive, return to the Navigation Grid to continue your adventure.

~ 37 ~

Suddenly you become aware of a small blue orb floating in the passageway ahead of you. You recognise it as a Will-o'-the-wisp. Then before you can do anything it flies towards you, hits you and you are momentarily engulfed in a warm blue light. After it dissipates you find yourself feeling refreshed.

Roll the die to see how many Health Points it bestows on you and then continue your adventure by returning to the Navigation Grid.

~ 38 ~

You suddenly find yourself facing down an angry looking Dwarf brandishing a war-hammer. You must fight your way past him.

Dwarf's Combat Skill	9
Dwarf's Combat Total	
My Combat Skill	
My Combat Total	

If you survive, you search his body and find two meals. You may also take his war-hammer. Roll the die once - this is the amount the weapon will add to your Combat Skill; in addition it will also reduce any damage you take in combat by 1 point.

Alter your Adventure Chart accordingly and then return to the Navigation Grid to continue your adventure.

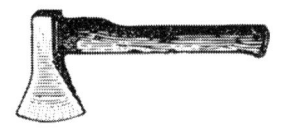

~ 39 ~

The passageway abruptly splits into two. You opt to take the right fork.

Return to the Navigation Grid to continue your adventure.

~ 40 ~

With sheer relief and exhaustion you sink to your knees next to the body of the defeated Baron and take a few moments to recover yourself. Then, without warning, the Baron's body is engulfed in a strange red mist and the chamber around you starts to shake. You realise, with horror, that his death has set off some kind of chain reaction and that the entire catacomb will soon be destroyed. Quickly you jump to your feet and make for the archway that you entered in from. However, just as you reach it, it collapses sealing you inside.

You curse your ill fortune, and Magnus who sent you on this mission in the first place. Then, just as you dodge out of the way of a large piece of stone that falls from the ceiling, you suddenly become aware that the Translocation Stone, which is still in your possession, is now glowing and the chamber around you seems to shimmer and then fade; only to be replaced by a forest clearing in which stands a large circular stone tower. Just in front of the tower, seated at a stone table, Magnus is smoking a long pipe. On seeing you he stands and a wily smile spreads across his face, knowing that because you are here you have completed your mission and that Baron Braxe is truly defeated. He beckons you over, pointing to the table. Waiting for you is your reward of the leather pouch filled with gold and gems, and also a large bowl of steaming stew which you rightly presume, this time, is indeed boar.

Printed by Amazon Italia Logistica S.r.l.
Torrazza Piemonte (TO), Italy